MARTIN
HANDFORD

WALKER BOOKS
LONDON

HI, FRIENDS!

MY NAME IS WALLY.
I'M JUST SETTING OFF ON A WORLD-
WIDE HIKE. YOU CAN COME TOO.
ALL YOU HAVE TO DO IS FIND ME,
WHEREVER I GO.

I'VE GOT ALL I NEED–WALKING
STICK, KETTLE, MALLET, CUP,
RUCKSACK, SLEEPING BAG,
BINOCULARS, CAMERA, SNORKEL,
BELT, BAG AND SHOVEL.

BY THE WAY, I WAS IN TOWN TODAY
AND I SAW A WINDOW CLEANER
DROP A BUCKET ON A MAN'S HEAD.
TERRIFIC!

FIND ME, IF YOU CAN.

Wally

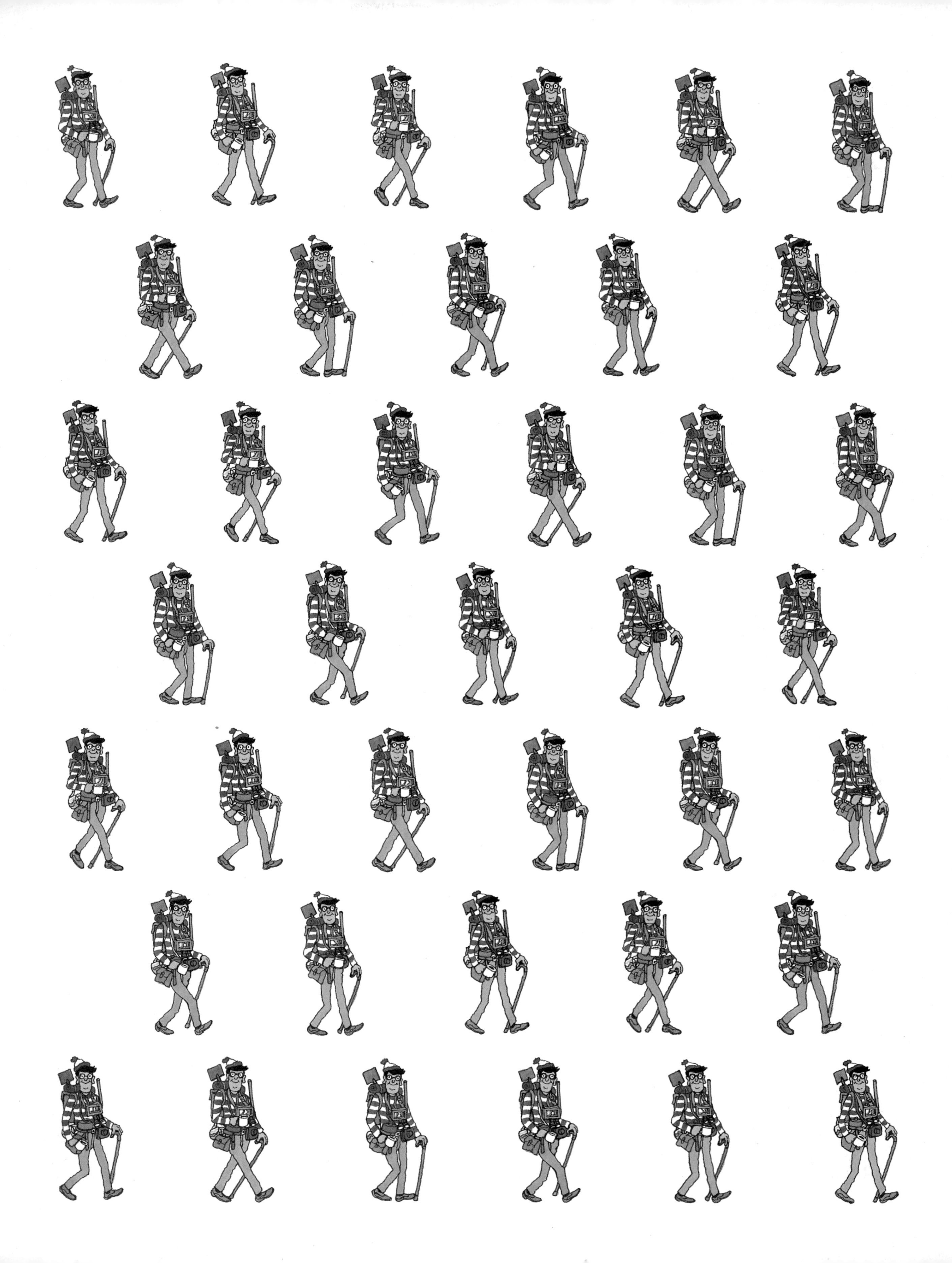

For Wally

First published 1987 by Walker Books Ltd
184-192 Drummond Street, London NW1 3HP

First printed 1987

Printed and bound by L.E.G.O., Vicenza, Italy

British Library Cataloguing in Publication Data
Handford, Martin
Where's Wally?
I. Title II. Lloyd, David, *1945-*
741 PZ7

ISBN 0-7445-0413-9

GREETINGS,
WALLY FOLLOWERS!
WOW, THE BEACH WAS
GREAT TODAY! I SAW
THIS GIRL STICK AN
ICE CREAM IN HER
BROTHER'S FACE, AND
THERE WAS A SAND
CASTLE WITH A REAL
KNIGHT IN ARMOUR
INSIDE! FANTASTIC!
Wally
WHERE'S
ON THE BEACH
WALLY?
TO:
WALLY FOLLOWERS,
HERE, THERE,
EVERYWHERE.

YODEL-ODEL-EE,
WALLY'S GANG!
I WALKED ACROSS THE SKI SLOPES TODAY AND SAW SOME INCREDIBLE SIGHTS! THERE WAS THIS SKIER GIVING FLOWERS TO HIS GIRLFRIEND, AND ANOTHER WITH AN ANCHOR OVER HIS SHOULDER, AND ONE ALL ROLLED UP IN A SNOWBALL! WOW! INCREDIBLE!
KEEP LOOKING FOR ME!
Wally
WHERE'S WALLY?
SKI SLOPES
TO:
WALLY'S GANG,
UPSTAIRS,
DOWNSTAIRS,
ALL OVER THE PLACE.

WHERE'S CAMP SITE WALLY?

WAKEY, WAKEY, WALLY FANS!
HAVE YOU EVER SEEN
MERMAIDS IN A CANAL?
OR A DOG WEARING INDIAN
FEATHERS? OR A FOOTBALL
KICKED RIGHT THROUGH A
CARAVAN? I HAVE. TODAY.
IT WAS JUST AMAZING!

WHERE AM I?

Wally

TO:
WALLY FANS,
NORTH OF THE SOUTH POLE,
EAST OF THE WEST POLE,
THE WORLD.

HUFF, PUFF, WALLY SPOTTERS!
I LOVE RAILWAY STATIONS,
DON'T YOU? THERE WAS SO
MUCH GOING ON TODAY —
COWS ESCAPING FROM TRUCKS,
A MAN ASLEEP BETWEEN
THE RAILS, DOGS CAUSING
ALL SORTS OF TROUBLE!
IT WAS REALLY WILD!
CAN YOU SEE ME?
Wally
WHERE'S WALLY? RAILWAY STATION
TO:
WALLY SPOTTERS,
ACROSS THE SEA,
DOWN THE ROAD,
ROUND THE BEND.

IT'S ME AGAIN, WALLY FOLKS!
SOME VERY STRANGE THINGS
WERE HAPPENING AT THE
AIRPORT THIS MORNING.
A HELICOPTER CHOPPED ALL
THE FLAGPOLES DOWN;
A SMUGGLER WAS CAUGHT
HIDING WATCHES IN HIS
BEARD; A HERD OF ELEPHANTS
WAS GETTING ONTO A JUMBO.
WEIRD!
I'M OUT THERE, SOMEWHERE.
Wally
WHERE'S
AIRPORT
WALLY?
TO:
WALLY FOLKS,
UNDER THE CARPET,
UNDER THE BED,
DOWN UNDER.

WHERE'S WALLY?
SPORTS STADIUM
ON YOUR MARKS,
WALLY CHAMPIONS!
WHAT A SPORTS DAY!
WHAT A RIOT!
LOOK AT THAT UMPIRE
PINNED DOWN BY JAVELINS!
LOOK AT THAT POLE VAULTER
BREAKING HIS POLE!
LOOK AT THAT VERY TALL
HIGH JUMPER! LOOK AT ME!
Wally
TO:
WALLY CHAMPIONS,
ONCE UPON A TIME,
YESTERDAY'S WORLD,
TOMORROW.

HOW-DE-DOO, WALLY SCHOLARS!
I'M CLEVER, AS YOU KNOW.
I GO TO MUSEUMS TO LEARN
THINGS. TODAY I FOUND OUT
ABOUT TICKLING THE TOES OF
A MAN IN THE STOCKS; ABOUT
KNOCKING DOWN A SUIT OF
ARMOUR; ABOUT THE
EGYPTIAN MUMMY'S BABY.
NOW THAT'S LEARNING!
HAVE YOU LEARNT TO FIND ME?
Wally
WHERE'S WALLY? MUSEUM
TO:
WALLY SCHOLARS,
AT SCHOOL,
IN TROUBLE,
AGAIN.

WHERE'S
AT SEA
ANCHORS AWAY, WALLY MATES!
WELL, SUCH WONDERS I SAW
AT SEA, AHOY, AHOY! A LOBSTER
ON A FLOATING BED! A CAPSIZED
DESERT ISLAND! A SHARK IN
A SWIMMING POOL! THE ONLY
QUESTION IS, CAN YOU SEA ME?
HA-HA!
Wally
TO:
WALLY MATES,
DOWN THE PLUGHOLE,
UP THE CREEK.

WATCH IT, WALLY HUNTERS!
I'M AN ANIMAL LOVER, THAT'S
FOR SURE. I LOVE THAT HIPPO
WITH ITS ALARM CLOCK; THAT
LION HAVING ITS MANE COMBED;
THE HAT-EATING GIRAFFE; THE
OWLS IN SPECTACLES. GREAT!
NOW TRACK ME DOWN, IF YOU
DARE.
Wally
WHERE'S WALLY?
SAFARI PARK
TO:
WALLY HUNTERS,
NICE PLACE,
THE JUNGLE,
OUTSIDE.

WOTCHA, WALLY WATCHERS!
SAW SOME TRULY TERRIFIC
SIGHTS TODAY – SOMEONE
BURNING TROUSERS WITH
AN IRON; A LONG THIN MAN
WITH A LONG THIN TIE;
A GLOVE ATTACKING A MAN.
PHEW! INCREDIBLE!

Wally

TO:
WALLY WATCHERS,
OVER THE MOON,
THE WILD WEST,
NOW.

ROLL UP, WALLY FUN LOVERS!
MAYBE YOU NOTICED ALREADY,
AND MAYBE YOU DIDN'T – BUT
I'VE LOST ALL MY THINGS.
NOW WE ALL HAVE TO GO BACK
TO THE BEGINNING, AND FIND
OUT WHAT I LOST AND WHERE
IT IS – ONE THING IN EVERY PLACE.
WOW!

TO:
WALLY FUN LOVERS,
BACK TO THE BEGINNING,
START AGAIN, TERRIFIC.

THE GREAT WHERE'S WALLY? CHECK LIST

Hundreds more things for Wally watchers to watch out for!

IN TOWN

- A dog on a roof
- A man on a fountain
- A man about to trip over a dog's lead
- A car crash
- A keen barber
- People in a street, watching TV
- A puncture caused by a Roman arrow
- A tearful tune
- A boy attacked by a plant
- A waiter who isn't concentrating
- A robber who's been clobbered
- A face on a wall
- A man coming out of a man-hole
- A man feeding pigeons
- A bicycle crash

SKI SLOPES

- A man reading on a roof
- A flying skier
- A runaway skier
- A backward skier
- A portrait in snow
- An illegal fisherman
- A snowball in the neck
- Two unconscious skiers
- Two skiers hitting trees
- An Alpine horn
- A snow skier
- A flag collector
- Two very scruffy skiers
- A skier up a tree
- A water skier on snow
- A Yeti
- A skiing reindeer
- A roof jumper
- A heap of skaters

THE RAILWAY STATION

- A boy falling from a train
- A break-down on tracks
- Naughty children on a train roof
- People being knocked over by a door
- A man about to step on a ball
- Three different times at the same time
- A wheelbarrow pram
- A face on a train
- Five people reading one newspaper
- A struggling bag carrier
- A show-off with suitcases
- A man losing everything from his cases
- A smoking train
- A squeeze on a bench
- A dog tearing a man's trousers
- Fare dodgers
- A hand caught between doors
- A cattle stampede
- A man breaking a weighing machine

ON THE BEACH

- A dog biting a boy's bottom
- A man who is overdressed
- A muscular medallion man
- A popular girl
- A water skier on water
- A stripy photo
- A punctured lilo
- A donkey who likes ice-cream
- A man being squashed
- A punctured beach ball
- A human pyramid
- A human stepping-stone
- Two odd friends
- A cowboy
- A human donkey
- Age and beauty
- A boy who follows in his father's footsteps
- Two men with vests, one without
- A boy being tortured by a spider
- A show-off with sandcastles
- A gang of hat robbers
- An Arab making pyramids
- Three protruding tongues
- Two oddly fitting hats
- An odd couple
- Five sprinters
- A towel with a hole in it
- A punctured hovercraft
- A boy who's not allowed any ice-cream

CAMP SITE

- A bull in a hedge
- Bull horns
- A shark in a canal
- A bull seeing red
- A careless kick
- Tea in a lap
- A low bridge
- People knocked over by a mallet
- A man surprised undressing
- A bicycle tyre about to be punctured
- Camper's camels
- A scarecrow that doesn't work
- A wigwam
- Large biceps
- A collapsed tent
- A smoking barbecue
- A fisherman catching old boots
- A winning penny-farthing
- Boy scouts making fire
- A roller hiker
- A man blowing up a boat
- A camper's butler
- Runners on a road
- A bull chasing children
- Scruffy campers
- Thirsty walkers

SPORTS STADIUM

- Three pairs of feet, sticking out of sand
- A cowboy starting races
- Hopeless hurdlers
- Ten children with fifteen legs
- A record thrower
- A shot-put juggler
- An ear trumpet
- A vaulting horse
- A runner with two wheels
- A parachuting vaulter
- A Scotsman with a caber
- An elephant pulling a rope
- People being knocked over by a hammer
- A gardener
- Three frogmen
- A nude runner
- A bed
- A bandaged boy
- A runner with four legs
- A sunken jumper
- A man with an odd pair of legs
- A man chasing a dog, chasing a cat
- A boy squirting water